Scrivener Jones is a journalist for *The Seattle Picayune,*
living in and reporting from the town of Kahnaway,
deep in the middle of the Olympic Peninsula.

Some birds appear to have an inate ability to navigate
the world via magnetic waves, a trait which some
people seem to possess. Scrivener is not one of those
people, though she is pretty good at finding her keys.

Kahnaway — pt18
Two Trails

Castor Maléfique Park + Signal Searching

by P. Calavara

Castor Maléfique Park

There's this thing I do and I can't figure out why. While at the grocery store, I'll carefully, even cautiously, pack all the groceries into their bags — being mindful to not break the eggs, smash the bread, or bruise the fruit, and then, once they're bagged, I'll treat them as invulnerable. It's like, after they're packed up, something clicks over in my mind and I act as if the thin cloth or paper sack will protect the food from any possible damage occurring, as I toss them willy-nilly into the car, paying no heed to the fragility of the contents. As I stood in my kitchen, contemplating the shattered and broken food before me, I wondered if there was a word for this sort of behavior, and, if there wasn't, if we could name it after me.[1]

The police scanner chirped out an emergency call for police and paramedics to respond to some sort of stabbing, thankfully changing my immediate concerns from home to work. I crammed the smashed bags of leaking groceries into the fridge to be future-Scrivener's problem, grabbed my work bag, and made

---

[1] This could be tricky, since *scrivening* and *jonesing* are both already things... so we might have go with something like *jivening* or *scronesing*. How about *scrijovening*?

my way back out to the car for what would turn out to be a pretty standard assault by battle axe.

The incident was at Castor Maléfique Park, which is a mixed-use park on the far east side of town, with a playground and various fields by a parking lot, then a fair-sized forest winding out behind it. The forest was honeycombed by trails, and for many kids, myself included, running madly along those paths in epic games of tag, hide-and-seek, capture-the-flag, or flee-the-pigman, would end up as our first real experience of being lost in the woods. About a third of a mile up the main trail was the *original* Castor Maléfique Park, a lovely open space hidden amongst the trees, perfect for picnics or whatever. This was where the authorities had been called to, and was no doubt where the killer whale that blazed past me, sirens blazing, was heading — while I was left far behind, forced to slowly make my way through stoplights and speed limits. That was fine. I never want to actually *beat* the police to the scene of a potentially in-progress incident. It happens on occasion, and usually necessitates me needing to hide in my car, run for my life, or, in one memorable case, engage in a ceremonial Puerto Rican-style knife fight with a Hessian.

The large grass space that made up the lower half of Castor Maléfique Park was currently divided up into several small soccer fields for the kiddie set, and I arrived just in time to see the tides part as the games halted long enough for a duo of paramedics to hustle across the fields with their gurney. I parked as they disappeared into the dense woods beyond the grass. The soccer players and parents did not give me the same respect they had given the paramedics, and I had to pick my way through the labyrinth of people and soccer, while dodging balls and fielding questions from concerned parents wanting to know what was happening. Unfortunately, I didn't have anything to tell them. At that point nobody really yet knew what was happening. Someone was injured. Something about an axe.

I finally reached the trailhead and hustled my way up it, fairly confident that I remembered the right trail to take through the maze of uneven paths crisscrossing through the woods. I guess I chose correctly, since I quickly caught up with the large, wheeled ambulance gurney barely a hundred feet in, around the first couple of corners.

The paramedic, a man named Jorge whom I was familiar with, had stopped to look at a victim, who was angrily protesting his attentions, in spite of a fair amount of blood gushing from his face.

"Quit it! I'm fine! They need you," the man argued vociferously. At least I think it was a man. He had green skin, a large angry mane, and a single pointed ear to go with a smashed nose that was bleeding everywhere, but I was pretty sure that I was looking at a guy, not an actual orc. Besides the theatrical makeup, he was dressed in a raggedy black robe and adorned in what looked like armored gauntlets. He also had a large sword strapped to his back and was holding an ornate wooden staff. I guess he hadn't been able to find his hobnail boots, because he was wearing Air Jordans.

"Buddy, you are injured!" Jorge insisted as he tried to look at the orc's face. He saw me coming and called to me. "Scrivener! Help me tell this guy he needs medical attention!"

"I'm fine," the orc insisted.

"I dunno, Jorge," I said. "He seems fine."

"Are you all insane? His fucking nose is broken!" Jorge closed his eyes in frustration.

"He's got a point," I told the orc. "Your nose looks pretty broken."

"No shit, Sherlock," the orc snapped, before pausing. "Pardon me, but I am aware that I am injured. I only insist that there is another, far more injured than myself who requires your assistance."

"¡Dios mío! Why not just say that then?"

"Well, I was trying."

"Whatever. You need to see a doctor, but don't drive anywhere, since there's a good chance you're concussed," Jorge said. "There's another ambulance on the way, promise you'll let them take a look at you."

"Yes, sir," said the orc, but I couldn't tell if he was being sarcastic or not.

"Have fun scaring soccer kids," I said to him.

"Hey, help me with this," Jorge said to me as he gestured to the other side of the large ambulance gurney. "Thanks. It's not meant for off-roading."

I grabbed it and we started to hot foot it up the trail as quickly as we could. "Where's your partner? Are you with Alexis today?"

"Yeah, but she ran on ahead while I stopped to check out that guy."

A chorus of children screaming back on the field rose through the trees. I guessed this meant that the armed, bloodied orc dressed in full fantasy-battle regalia had stepped from the woods towards the soccer games. I chuckled. "It's the little things in life, right?"

"You are a crazy person, Ms. Jones," I could hear Jorge rolling his eyes at me, even though I couldn't see them.

"So any idea what's going on?"

"Something to do with an axe and a stabbing, but not really more than that," replied Jorge. "Hey — what was the deal with that guy? Why was he all dressed like a, uh… un mago. Shit, what's the word. Like in those hobbit movies."

"An orc? A wizard?"

"Yeah. Why was he dressed like a wizard?"

"He had green skin and you're curious about why he was wearing robes?" I chuckled as we hustled along the trail. "Okay, so there are a bunch of people who role-play up here sometimes. They're called *LARPers.* Have you ever heard of that?"

"*LARPers?* No. Should I have?"

"I mean… no, probably not. It's an acronym, LARP, or L-A-R-P, for Live Action Role Play. It's like a Dungeons-and-Dragons-adjacent type thing," I tried to explain.

"Dungeons and Dragons? Ha! Shit, I played that as a kid, but we never hit each other with axes. Just dice and sometimes our fists."

"Yeah, like, normal board game fights, right?" I laughed. "Well, sometimes these guys get dressed up as their characters and then play out their stories and fight in real life."

"Sounds hardcore," said Jorge, impressed.

"Well, they usually use foam swords and stuff, not real ones."

"Oh, well, maybe I'll stick with my fight club, then," Jorge snickered and I couldn't tell if he was kidding or not. Was there a fight club in Kahnaway? Did people even still do that sort of thing?

We finished heaving the gurney up the last bit of the trail to a large clearing in the woods. This was the original site of Castor Maléfique Park — a roughly half-acre of land that was mostly cleared of trees, broken up by huge rocks big enough to climb up. There was a fairly popular picnic shelter, some hundred year old play equipment, the wreckage of an old log cabin, and a creepy, fog-shrouded pond that disappeared off into the woods at the far end. There were also about twenty people dressed in fantasy medieval regalia, made from hammered metal, carefully shaped foam, and artfully taped cardboard. There were also a couple guys that were basically wearing shipping boxes spray painted grey, but everyone starts somewhere — there was no judgement here.

Jorge immediately left me with the gurney and rushed over to help his fellow paramedic, Alexis, who was furiously trying to administer medical attention to a giant of a man who was bleeding, like, a really ridiculous amount from his side.

Officers Grant and Carol were the responding police officers on scene, and they were standing beside a short, somewhat stocky, bloodied woman with a grim expression on her face. Grant saw me, and hurried over to help me push the heavy gurney the final way over the uneven ground, to get it beside the paramedics as they worked.

In spite of having a fair amount of the victim's blood on himself, I noted with some satisfaction that Grant was looking less gaunt than he had in a while — my program of forcing him to cram food into himself was having the desired effect. I knew that he was still caught up with *The Church Of The King* mushroom cult, but malnutrition was a trick to blind servitude, not a path to escape, so first things first. We would start with strong-in-body, then move on to strong-in-mind.

I brought my focus back to the job at hand, and looked down at the man writhing in pain before us on the ground. He had been chopped nearly in two from his left side, and his face was twisted almost beyond recognition as the morphine attempted to kick in before leaking out. He was one of the few people there wearing actual metal armor, which looked really expensive, and he had taken a fair amount of time painting scales all over his exposed skin. There was obviously a ridiculous amount of blood around his midsection, and it smelled like a stomach. "Is that dude a dragon wearing armor?" I spoke my thoughts aloud.

"You're all fucking nuts..." replied Jorge.

"Can we help at all?" asked Grant.

"Not really... Just keep the lookie-loos away. Another crew is already on their way up the trail,"

Alexis said as she worked to somehow strap the man's top half back to his bottom half.

Grant nodded, and turned to the crowd, "Back it up! Back it up! We need space! We'll take statements shortly, so get your stories straight now."

"Get your stories straight?" I asked him and tried not to smirk, as he gestured to the crowd of paladins and elves and red mages and stuff.

"It just came out," he smirked, a little embarrassed.

I looked back at the massive wound in the side of the prone man, and asked a question that had been bugging me. "That's real armor, right? That looks like metal, not foam or cardboard." I gestured at the heavy mix of chain mail and plate metal adorning the man's chest and shoulders.

"It is," said Alexis. "It's a pain in the ass to work around."

"Okay, so I gotta ask… why go to all this work to wear all this armor, but then leave your midsection exposed?"

"Isn't that just how kids are wearing their armor these days?" Alexis asked sarcastically.

The man looked up at me through glazed eyes, with a mouthful of blood and agony. "Abs…" he managed to say, "Abs… looked too good… not to…"

"Oh. Well. Okay then," I replied, still feeling nonplussed. "So… stab in the dark here, but that's our weapon, yeah?" I pointed to a large, ornate, blood-and-gore-covered double-headed battle axe laying on the ground nearby.

"Well, nobody has confirmed it, but that seems about right," nodded Grant.

Before I could reply, a new voice of authority carried across the park.

"Hey, hey, *heyyyyywhatthefuck?*" Officer Chuck née Charles's eyes widened and jaw dropped as he entered the clearing at the top of the trail. He was followed by two more paramedics who immediately rushed over to help Alexis and Jorge. Officer Chuck gave himself a moment to hold back his lunch, taking deeps breaths, before turning back to us. "They called this in as a *stabbing?*"

"Hey, Chuck," I greeted the police officer.

"Can you handle the crowd?" Grant asked Chuck, as he looked back towards Officer Carol and the cuffed prisoner. "Our perp's a little squirrely."

"Uh, yeah, sure." Chuck turned to the crowd of knights, rogues, and rangers milling about and tried to herd them away from the action. "All of you, over here now. Okay, huddle up, come on, come on. Okay, now, which of you want to see me practice my close-up magic, and which of you want to get booked into stir for not *loving* my close-up magic?"

"Close-up magic?" I asked Grant, as we crossed the clearing back over towards Carol.

"His daughter got him a book for Christmas, and now we all must suffer."

"Hey Scrivener. You ever seen a half-dwarf-half-elf before?" asked Officer Carol as we walked up to her and what I assume was the assailant. Sitting on the ground, with her hands clapped in irons, was a woman in her twenties — blood spattered, pointy ears, foam armor that couldn't decide what style it wanted to be, and either a quality wig or huge, Irish-red hair pulled into a wild braid.

"Hello, Officer Carol," I greeted the cop. "A half-dwarf, half-elf? Is that even a thing?"

The woman spat on the ground at my feet, "Obviously it is! You're as bad as that fucking dragonborn. We are called Dwelves, and though we are few, we are proud!"

"Oh. Sorry, I didn't mean any offense. I was proclaiming my ignorance on the subject, not belittling anyone," I apologized to the Dwelf.

The Dwelf growled, but I guess she accepted my apology as she didn't say anything more about it.

"Do we have a name yet?" Grant asked Carol.

"Still just the one," Carol replied.

"I am *Gimolas the Authenticator!*" the Dwelf declared, rattling her handcuffs menacingly. She turned to me and stared into my soul with steely eyes, "That's Gimolas with an *I*."

"Got it," I nodded.

"Do you guys do this sort of thing up here a lot?" Carol asked Gimolas. "It's a great location for it."

"We battle where the battle takes us," Gimolas declared.

"What was this place called? Caster Park?" Carol looked around at the setting with approval.

"Castor Maléfique Park," Grant said. "Though I don't know why it's called that. Sounds French." He looked at me, "How about you? You're usually useful for this sort of thing."

"I feel like you're calling me a nerd, Officer Grant." I looked to Gimolas, "Is he calling me a nerd?"

"Foolish human — don't bother me with your petty squabbles," Gimolas was smoldering. "I must soon find a way to escape these paltry shackles to finish the job I started with that dragonborn."

"That dude was a dragonborn? Damn," Carol said, impressed. "I thought they were made of sterner stuff."

"I'm not calling you a nerd, Scriv'. I'm calling you… a fount of useful information," Grant explained.

I sighed. "Castor Maléfique *is* French. It means 'evil beaver,' making this Evil Beaver Park."

"Really? I think that's the same name as an all-girls reform school back where I grew up that I begged my parents to send me to," Carol said, wistfully.

I let out a curt laugh. "Well, in this case, the legend is supposedly about *actual* beavers, who murdered a group of French furriers that had set up camp here to hunt and trap, what else, beavers. The story goes that the beavers dropped some trees on them, but also just, y'know, chewed their legs off and then murdered them. Supposedly they live in that haunted pond back there that always seems to be covered in mist."

"Neat," said Carol. "Wholesome."

"Yeah, I'm pretty sure Disney has an option on making it a movie."

"You have *got* to be screwing with us," Grant said. "Right?"

"Hey — I don't make up the crazy stuff, I just report it." I solemnly put my hand over my heart.

"Well, what about the D.B. Cooper Underground stuff?" Grant put his hands on his hips and narrowed his eyes at me. "You made *all* that stuff up."

"Oh, yeah. Well… you can't count that shit against me," I shrugged.

"Why not?"

"Because I made that stuff up for money," I solemnly explained.

"What are you two even talking about?" asked Carol, perplexed. "That underground tour thing?"

"I'll explain it to you later," Grant sighed, before remembering that he had a job to do here. He turned to Gimolas. "So. Why did you chop that guy in half?"

"You humans could not possibly understand the inner turmoil that we Dwelves feel, always at war with ourselves. Creatures torn and hewn from two lineages full of nothing but hatred and distrust for each other," Gimolas stormed.

"If you're at war with *yourself*, then what was your problem with that dragon-dude?" Officer Carol looked at her armored culprit and pressed, gesturing over towards the man being tended to by the team of paramedics.

"The dragonborn was a speciesist fool, arrogant and cruel in his taunts, and so, to silence his dark, lying tongue, I clove him in twain," replied the Dwelf, with gestures as epic as the handcuffs would allow.

"That sounded like a confession, have we Miranda'd this one, yet?" asked Carol.

"I demandeth to be provided with a lawyer or some other demonic persona to take up my case and advise me," shouted Gimolas.

"Demandeth? Is that even a word?" Grant side-eyed me.

"Oh, Officer Grant, *anything* can be a word if you truly believe in it and clap your hands," I explained lovingly.

"Carol? Care to opine?" Grant asked.

"Naw, I'll let you two argue over semantics while I just stay here trying to do my job and investigate this nonsense like a real cop," Carol shook her head. "I mean, somehow a dragonborn was beaten in basic combat *without* the use of a magical weapon. It just doesn't add up."

Grant and I looked at her, perplexed, but could not put together an explanation.

The paramedics had somehow stabilized the big guy, which seemed miraculous given how much of him had been chopped in two, and it took the assistance of both Officers Chuck née Charles and Grant to help transport him onto the gurney — it wasn't just the size of the man, but the heavy metal chain mail and the plated armor.

"This is bullshit," grunted Alexis as the six of them heaved. "How is it that the one guy *not* wearing cardboard and foam gets chopped in half?"

"Why couldn't you just cut it off?" wondered Chuck.

"We don't usually carry bolt cutters in our first aid kits," Jorge replied.

"How about the jaws of life?" Chuck offered. "I think I have some back in my trunk."

"He'd be long dead before then," Jorge said.

"I think my pocket knife has a can opener," Alexis replied.

With the victim loaded up onto the gurney, the four paramedics began the arduous trip back down the trail with the poor man, who I'm sure felt every single bump in spite of the painkillers that were coursing through his body.

Officer Chuck handed a notepad over to Grant. "Here're the names and contact info of all the witnesses."

Grant looked at the list with a cocked eyebrow. "Qirora Flalphinthronn? Dunvernin the Lightbringer? Kristov Fuentes. Chuck, most of these are fake names."

"*Character* names," Chuck corrected him, "Look, man, if you want something different, *you* talk to them. Apparently when most of these people role-play, they go method."

"Christ. Whatever," Grant rolled his eyes.

I took a real look at the crowd of people and realized that I knew a couple of them. Does that say something about me? I caught the eye of a large person of Pacific Island descent and gestured for them to come over. They stepped around the other costumed adventurers and sheepishly stepped over to me. Their name was Manny, and they were dressed in silver leathers, with pieces of foam armor attached here and there. There was a foam sword slung across their back, and there were bloodstains all over their hands and forearms from helping the injured man. They had tried half-heartedly to clean themselves, but the evidence remained.

"Hey, Manny."

"Uh… Hi, Scrivener," they looked shell-shocked, their eyes red and puffy, as they tried to look small but failed. Manny owned *Manny's Tow & Surf,* the tow truck company that serviced the region.

"What are you?" I asked.

"Elven paladin," they mumbled, sheepishly, as Officer Carol joined us.

"Manny, right?" asked Carol.

"Um, yeah. Hi."

"What's your name here?"

"Uh, Wynandoral."

"Nice. Paladin, right? So you have to tell the truth," said Carol. "What's the deal with Gimolas over there?"

"She's fine, or, uh…" Manny tried to backtrack, "at least she always has been previously. I mean, she's got a hot temper, for sure, and not just in roleplaying, but nothing ever like this before."

"A real axe, though?" asked Carol.

"Yeah, it, uh… it wasn't hers. It's actually Dennis's axe."

"Dennis?" I asked.

Carol clarified, "The guy who got chopped in half. Dennis Orban. I can't remember his dragon name. Grant said it — something something the Burninator?"

"Lildathaaller Eraxoros of the Burning," clarified Manny.

"Oh. Well. I was close," Carol shrugged.

"He brought that axe, but it's just for show. He's had it a few times now, but doesn't actually use it in combat, he just usually shows off how heavy and fancy it is while swinging it around doing tricks. He's got more muscles than manners." Manny looked at their shoes, highly detailed, complex things made of leather that wrapped up to the knees.

"Anything you can tell us about him?" I asked. "Have he and Gimolas had any issues before?"

"They have, yeah, because he's a huge asshole," Manny said, before slapping their hand over their mouth. "Shit. I can't believe I said that… uh …Is he going to die?"

Carol shook her head, "I've got no idea."

I put a reassuring hand on Manny's shoulder. "Hey, just because something bad happens to someone doesn't mean they're somehow magically not assholes."

"I guess that's good, cause I fucking hate that guy. Not that I wanted this to actually happen to him, though I'd be lying if I didn't say we *all* fantasize about basically this exact thing happening. No respect for pronouns, and not a time do I see him when he doesn't give me shit about my size. He always, *always*, calls me a giant or an orc or some shit, and never lets me just be a damned elf," Manny told us, letting some anger out.

"So what I'm hearing is that he was being an asshole, then the Dwelf over there took his axe and chopped him in two?" Carol asked.

"I mean, I wasn't within earshot, but that's what it looked like," Manny said, "I could see them talking during a break, then it looked like she just took the axe from his hands, all calm like, said something, and then: *WHACK!*"

"Then you called 9-1-1?" Carol asked. "Or, well, someone did?"

"Actually, she did — Gimolas did. She actually pulled out *his* phone and called while we were still sorta realizing what was happening. She was hanging up as I got to them," said Manny.

"That is going to be one hell of a recording," mumbled Carol.

"What happened to the wizard-orc with the broken nose?" I asked.

"Who, Jim? He fell — tripped on a root while running over with the rest of us to see what had happened," Manny shrugged.

"Hey, Wynandoral?" We were interrupted by a thin male voice and looked over to see a man who could only have been a necromancer. "Did you tell them about the curse?"

"Oh, uh, no… I didn't," Manny replied.

"Curse?" Carol asked.

"That axe is cursed," the necromancer said pointedly, poking a mean-looking metal staff into Carol's personal space, before using it to gesture at the axe that was still laying over in the grass. "This isn't its first victim."

"And you are…?" Carol asked.

"Darkcrux the Redominator," the necromancer crossed his arms dramatically, nearly braining me with his staff as he did.

"Uh, like, your real name, your legal name," Carol said.

"Yeah," Darkcrux nodded, "I know." He reached deep into his black cloak, and pulled out a skull-shaped wallet, then opened it and took out his driver's license.

Carol took it and I leaned over to get a look myself. "I'll be damned… *Darkcrux T. Redominator.* Hey Scrivener, is this dude like your cousin or something? How do you people end up with these names?"

"I took this name for myself," Darkcrux glowered evilly. "There is no reason to hide my true self from mere mortals."

Manny leaned over to Carol and me, and whispered, "Thaddeus Grodin. He's got a brother who works at the DOL in Lacey that did that up for him."

"Why would you even do that?" whined Darkcrux.

"I'm a Paladin. I'm forced to tell the truth," Manny solemnly intoned.

"Geez, Manny, you sometimes take this shit too seriously," Darkcrux the Redominator whined as Carol and I tried to stifle our laughter.

"So what's this about a cursed axe?" I inquired, barely able to contain myself.

"It chopped off some fingers a couple weeks ago," Manny conceded. "It was an accident."

"NO — it was the curse," Darkcrux hastily corrected. "Dennis found some bullshit reason to not make the last payment for the axe, so the blacksmith had a witch curse it."

"Dude, that was a storyline that Parappa the Bard made up *after* Belanas's fingers got cut off," Manny said, exasperated.

"No it wasn't. I mean, he *did* tell that story, but it was also the truth. Besides, how else do you explain him getting cut in half? *Curse.*"

"How else do you explain an asshole getting hit with an axe?" Manny was exasperated. "He was an asshole who got hit with an axe for being an asshole when there was an axe around. Last month you tried to hit him with your fucking staff. If you had had an axe, you would have tried to hit him with an axe. He inspires it."

"Lots of assholes *don't* get hit with axes. He inspires it *because he's cursed!*" Darkcrux was fuming.

"Wait," Carol interjected, "Is it the axe that's cursed, or is it him?"

Manny and Darkcrux both turned to her in unison, "Both."

This might have gone on had Grant not interrupted. "Carol? Can you come over here?"

"Sure," Carol responded before turning back to the necromancer and the paladin. "Pardon me, I need to go do cop shit." She smiled politely and then turned to walk back over to Grant.

"Thanks," I said to them. "We'll talk more later. Manny, we should get together for coffee and catch up again soon."

I followed Carol over to where Grant was standing beside Gimolas the Dwelf, who had a peculiar look on her face, which I couldn't quite place.

"So… you're telling me this is *not* a dream?" Gimolas's voice was slow and thoughtful.

"Nope," Grant shook his head.

"And you're *totally* sure about that?"

"Pretty sure," Grant said, though maybe not without some uncertainty, that he noticed me noticing.

"Well, *I'm* sure," Carol said, rolling her eyes at her fellow officer. "Top layer of the cake here."

"Huh." Gimolas looked from her shackled bloody hands over to where Officer Chuck née Charles was trying to figure out how to fit a bloodied four-foot battle axe with a massive double head into an evidence bag meant for a pistol. "So, I really, actually chopped Lildathaaller Eraxoros of the Burning in half with his own axe…"

"Seems so," Grant said.

"Well… He can't say he didn't have it coming," Gimolas muttered, totally free of remorse.

More officers from the Kahnaway PD showed up to help Officer Chuck corral the other witnesses and take statements, as Grant and Carol took their prisoner back down the trail to their waiting patrol car. I went with them in case she said anything newsworthy, but she mostly didn't talk, a glassy, taciturn look on her face as she trod down the trail. The soccer matches had ended for the day, but there were still dozens of kids and parents on the field, either slow to leave or for some reason still curious about the dragon-dude wearing armor who had been chopped in half.

As Grant opened the door to his cruiser and Carol helped the Dwelf into the vehicle, she paused, and looked up at me with deep eyes. "Remember," she said, with steel in her voice, "Gimolas with an *I*."

Grant closed the door, and the three of us stood there in silence, each wrestling with our own emotions and reactions to this crime.

Finally, Carol broke the silence, as she put her hands over her heart, "Someday I'm going to marry that girl."

As I headed back towards the trail and Castor Maléfique Park to try and dig up some more quotes for my article, I looked up to the sound of a helicopter, and saw the EMS medevac speeding east towards Seattle, no doubt holding both halves of a verified asshole. Several hours of emergency surgery later, Lildathaaller Eraxoros of the Burning, aka Dennis Orban, would be moved from critical to stable, and he would be released from the hospital a couple of weeks later, totally normal except that his top half now looked like it was perched at a jaunty angle atop his bottom half. Gimolas, whose real name turned out to be Rachel Coyne, apparently got *real* weird in jail, and so they ran a blood test which came back with something odd in it. Further investigation revealed that her water had been spiked with a hallucinogen, so maybe she had been dreaming after all.[2] It was enough that she was able to eventually cop a plea deal down to third degree assault with a small fine and forty hours of community service. Maybe she'd have seen some prison time if it

---

[2] I went at local semi-pro tripper Nouty Ned with a copy of the official toxicology report showing the breakdown of the drugs that they had found in her system, and he said it looked like a total bullshit molecule cobbled together from an internet search of psilocybin, coffee, and tryptophan. That said, he's also a grown man who calls himself Nouty Ned and said that if I could get him any of the drug, he would totally "hit that shit," so it's up to you how seriously to take anything he says.

hadn't turned out that Dennis Orban had bullied the judge's cousin relentlessly in middle school — there's probably a moral in there somewhere.

I did my best to get to the bottom of this, calling everyone who would answer their phone. I had so many unanswered questions! Who would or could have spiked the water? Was Rachel Coyne AKA Gimolas a victim or had she done it herself? What even had she been theoretically dosed with? Or maybe she hadn't been dosed with anything at all and it had all been a ploy to get away with chopping a dude in half. But, then, if that were the case, then who had helped her with the ruse — the water bottle, evidence, and bloodwork all vanished before it could be tested a second time. Was there a conspiracy or was it just incompetence? I wasn't willing to rule out either possibility. I did what I could, but in the end, nobody had any answers for me.

In fact, nobody but me seemed to think there was even a mystery here worth solving. Maybe she had been drugged, maybe she hadn't — it didn't change that some guy got chopped in half. For better or worse, that's where the story is going to have to end. Maybe I would have kept digging longer, and maybe I might even have found some resolution, had my editor not called me up to call me off it. Was that another part of the coverup? Had someone got to him or was it just that the story didn't have legs?

Or was it maybe because Dennis Orban's dad had called up my boss and demanded that I write a hit piece against the Dwelf? Take it for what it's worth, but the exact message my boss sent when he killed the story was, "If I read another single word about that fucking asshole and those elves, I'll find that axe myself and finish what they started."

Maybe it was evil beavers, or maybe there *was* a curse after all.

I guess we'll never know.

Kahnaway

Signal Searching

The sun beat down upon me whenever I stepped out of the shadow of the forest, only to disappear again a moment later as I slid back between the trees, enveloped once more in deep green darkness. It was forest primeval — overgrown, dense, ancient, and more ferns than I had thought could exist — until, suddenly, you would step out and come across a clear-cut section where loggers had been, or you would find ATV tracks, or the dead husk of a cabin. Particularly strange was a large saltwater fishing boat, long abandoned, a tree growing through the hull, somehow left here fifty years ago, far from any roads or bodies of water. The boat was even a marker on the map I was following. I had to bear left.

I was on a trail, or a series of trails, through the woods south of Olympic National Park, on property of uncertain ownership — could have been state-owned or tribal lands, could have been timber industry, could have been locals or crazies who bought up land cheap just to have a chunk of land somewhere.[1] Maybe it was pure wild out here, and nobody had claim to this land. It was an interesting thought, which I rolled around in for a while as I followed the map's directions. The map itself was a hand-drawn thing with crisp, tightly lettered instructions, and it had been left on my doorstep a week ago, with a note telling me to be there at this particular time and day.

Dr. Mag Kenney, internationally recognized as a foremost expert on mushrooms, had fallen off the edge of the world about a year before — a few months after I met her while doing an article on local legends. I had specifically been writing about the Kaisershroom, a mushroom that folklore would have us believe could telepathically control people to make them do its bidding. We had met on a trail not too dissimilar from the one I was on, and she had taken me on a tour through the woods, where she delivered a roving impromptu lecture on mushrooms. She answered my questions, but was dismissive of the Kaisershroom's existence and supposed powers, because who wouldn't be? It had been a delightful day, that had only taken a darker turn in my memory months later when it became apparent that Kahnaway had begun to be overtaken by a bizarre cult with a special focus on mushrooms, not too dissimilar to some of the legends of the Kaisershroom — as completely stupid and ridiculous as that sounds.

---

[1] Hey, I'm not judging. You're talking to a girl who owns 20+ acres of hilly scrubland 10 miles from nowhere in south-central Washington that she bought for a song on a whim in her mid-twenties. I don't know what I was thinking. Was I planning on camping there? Raising sheep? Starting a cult of my own? Who knows! But it's there if you ever want to go look for rattlesnakes with me.

I had tried to contact the doctor pretty much weekly since then, but had not heard back from her, as she ignored all my emails, phone calls, and carrier pigeons. I had finally decided to investigate why she had ghosted me around the time when bioluminescent holiday mushrooms had begun flooding the town, and had learned from a rotating cast of college administrators, grad students, and family members that she was 'out of country' doing research, though even this came with a cloud of mystery, with none of the people I spoke to agreeing on which continent she was researching in, nevermind what country. Nonetheless I had continued reaching out on the regular, figuring that wherever she was she would have internet access eventually, until finally, out of nowhere, this note and map had been delivered to my front door.

I don't need any lectures about how stupid it was to come out here alone. It hadn't been my first choice. Obviously I had tried to get a friend or companion to come with, but none had been able to, with one even having to cancel the morning of. It's like they've all got real jobs and lives or something. At any rate, I had no choice but to go it alone.

The birds were in full bloom, as late spring turned to summer, and I enjoyed their medley as I hiked through the woods and over the gentle hills, following the precise directions written on the map I had been sent.

I had taken Highway 13 to 101 to 8, to get here, then roads, and finally lumber roads until those petered out and I'd been forced to abandon my car and take to foot on the thin paths that snaked through this part of the world. Sometimes they seemed so slight you really had to use your imagination to see a trail at all, while other times they would widen out for a stretch and you would swear you were at a state park, about to take a turn and find yourself at a campground or a gift shop. I was armed only with the knife and bear spray I always kept on hand when I left the house,[2] having declined to take along the actual *sword* that a friend had tried to lend me when they heard I was coming out here alone. What the hell was I going to do with a sword?

The hike itself had been pleasant, though always with that undertone of terror that comes with hiking trails like this by myself — the concerns that you might run into a bear, or a chainsaw killer, or an illegal pot farm run by a murderous cartel of hillbillies.[3] I tried to keep my attention laser focused on potential threats, or on recognizing the various bird calls that drifted by on the breeze, but found my mind kept wandering back up the trail and down the road to Kahnaway and *The Church Of The King* — the mushroom death-cult that had bought and taken up residence in the old megachurch near the freeway. My editor had been loath to sign my checks for time spent investigating something as ludicrous as a mushroom cult, so most of the investigating and research I had done so far had been on my own dime, though I'd kept the receipts just in case. *Something* was going on, and at some point I would get paid to write about it. Assuming I didn't get eaten by a bear or a bigfoot on this trail first.

---

[2] For feral peacocks and wild pigs.

 [3] Scoff all you like, but I've encountered all three while hiking.

I'm not sure what I had expected to find where X marked the spot, but what I found was a dead body. Dr. Mag Kenney was laying hunched over unnaturally in the shade of a big-leaf oak tree, and I knew without needing to check that she wasn't just sleeping. Nonetheless, I immediately made my way across the clearing to her, and checked her for signs of life: breathing, a pulse, or a hot take about superhero movies. But all signs came back negative. Dr. Mag Kenney was dead.

Dead dead dead.

I sat on my haunches beside the dead body, as I tried to decide what to do while looking at the bronze-skinned, elderly woman who still had the body of a star athlete.

After a moment's consideration, I took out my cursed cellphone, and began waving it around in the air, as if I were trying to get a signal. This was entirely theater, as there was no way the cursed phone would have allowed me to summon help even if I had found a signal, but it did give me a good excuse to move around the clearing and give the place a good examination without looking like paranoia had eaten my soul. After waving my phone around willy nilly like an idiot, I finally decided that I was truly alone, and cursed out loud at the device, cramming it back into the pocket of my tactical capris. Next, I pulled out my camera, and took several photos of Dr. Kenney's lifeless body, documenting exactly how I had found her. There was no way to carry her back down to my car, so I laid her out flat on the ground, before quite respectfully searching her for injury or obvious cause of death, though I found nothing.

Next, I searched her belongings, even though it felt ghoulish, but found nothing out of the ordinary. I took photographs of her wallet, her journal, her phone, and her notebooks, before transferring all of these items into my own backpack. She had a rolled sleeping bag strapped atop her backpack, which I completely zipped her up in, as some sort of makeshift shroud to protect the body, though I knew it was feeble at best. I searched the undergrowth around the clearing, until I came across several random mushrooms, which I picked, and placed atop her chest on top of the sleeping bag. Finally, I kneeled over the body for a respectful moment of solemnity, before rising back up to head down the trail back to my car and the authorities.

I didn't make it too far back towards my car before suddenly deciding to stop. From there, I left the trail, turned around, and began heading back to the clearing secretly — in the bushes, behind the trees, from the shadow. I moved as silently as I could, which was louder than a bird or a squirrel, but not so loud as to draw more than a glance. Once I had made my way back to the clearing, I found a place set far enough away to sit back and see everything while remaining hopefully invisible through the green. And so I sat, and so I watched.

It's tough to believe something like a hypnotic mushroom or a telepathic toadstool could exist. Most people, most sane people, *might* be willing to believe in something more rational, like hotel lobby hypnotists and county fair psychics, maybe even a telepathic toad or some mesmeric stone fruit, but *a mushroom?* That defies credulity. The far more likely explanation was that *The Church Of The King* was just another regular-ass death cult,[4] which just happened to be mushroom themed — some charismatic leader overpromising on fungi-flavored eternal life.

Still.

This cult *did* seem to have something about it that was different than some of the other cults I've known, reported on, and gone undercover to investigate. For starters, members of this cult, including my friend Grant from the Kahnaway PD, seemed to be behaving in ways that were a little stranger than most other cult members I've dealt with before. I've known any number of cultists who enthused endlessly and could speak of nothing else but their great new religion, and I've known many cult members who steadfastly refused to acknowledge or discuss their cults, but I've never met so many cultists who seemed to whip from one extreme to the other, seemingly at random. These mushroom cultists just couldn't seem to get on the same page. Sometimes they evangelized, other times they didn't seem to know that they were even in a cult at all, depending on when you spoke with them. And whenever you tried to discuss the cult with them in detail — regardless of if they were trying to convince you to attend services or denying that they had ever heard of it — they would seem to begin experiencing some deeply rooted painful trauma that

---

[4] Death cults are, alarmingly, far more common than most people realize. You almost certainly know someone in one without realizing it, though they probably don't realize it either, so I guess that makes you even.

would prevent them from speaking. I mean... I *know* that hypnotic mushrooms are stupid, but *something* seemed to be doing a number on these people.

My first encounters with the mushroom cult had been about a year before, when my friend and local cop Officer Grant had led me out to an abandoned house deep in the woods. Some people had been congregating in a nearby park and then marching there in the middle of the night with candles. For some reason this skeeved out the neighbors, who had called it in, and Grant had been dispatched to investigate, after which he had decided that it might be something I would enjoy seeing and would maybe be able to spin an article out of. It *was* pretty creepy, with candles everywhere and a nice skeletal body on a La-Z-boy recliner with a strange mushroom in its rib cage, in a basement that looked as if it had been used for both rituals and maybe some kind of mushroom farming. Someone had hauled in a lot of fertilizer from somewhere for some reason, and coated the basement floor, which was still dotted with spores.

Not too long after that was when I noticed a change beginning in Officer Grant.

The next mushroom related activities were a couple of months later, when an organization called PilzKing came out of nowhere to purchase the empty megachurch and its associated retail establishment downtown, which they then converted into an upscale mushroom retailer, selling mushrooms, spores, and various "shroomlife" accoutrements. There was no story there at the time — churches come and go, and retail stores pop up like meerkats — so my editor had only allowed me about 15 minutes of time to look into it on the clock. As near as I could tell from glancing through financial records, internet sleuthing, and posting up at farmer's markets, PilzKing had started off with a huge amount of money made from selling an almost unheard of quantity of matsutake mushrooms, enough to wreck the market for the season while providing the organization with a stupid amount of money — enough to buy an empty megachurch and a business downtown. Not the usual financial seed for a cult, but here we are. From that point on, they had begun recruiting in earnest.

The Church Of The King grew quickly, with more and more people attending its irregularly scheduled services. The mushroom retail store served as something of a recruitment center, offering truly amazing things, like bioluminescent mushrooms and beauty spores, *for free* in exchange for attending a service — and it only seemed to take one visit for people to become hooked. The parking lot at the megachurch that housed the cult became more crowded every week, until they were forced to lease a second parking lot and shuttle people over. I had been inside the church once, before I really knew what it was, and that had been more than enough for me. It had been a bizarre place, dedicated to autumn and death, and I had felt a suffocating presence trying to take over my body as I had inhaled the sharp scents of decaying leaves and life. I had never before felt such a complete loss of control, and had barely made it outside.

Mushrooms that could control your mind. It was such a stupid and absurd idea.

I had been watching Dr. Mag Kenney's lifeless corpse for what felt like hours, but had actually only been about 45 minutes, and I was seriously starting to question my own sanity, when she finally stirred. The movement was subtle, a flick of movement on the sleeping bag here or there, then nothing, then a shuffle, then nothing, then finally a deep gasp of breath. I watched silently as the woman pulled her way out of the sleeping bag, as if she were made of wood. She lay there for a moment shivering, before her eyes began darting around. She saw the mushrooms that I had left on her body in memoriam, and managed to grab them, eating them like a squirrel, no thumbs and tiny quick nibbles.[5] After that she lay back down for a few minutes. Finally, she sat back up, and opened her backpack with stiff fingers, fighting the zipper until she could pull out a water bottle. She furiously drank the water, before pulling out a second bottle, and draining that one in the same fashion. After that she lay back down and stared at the sky for several minutes. Eventually she clambered back up to her feet, moved to the side of the clearing, and threw up.

I'm not sure how to describe what I was feeling as I watched this all unfold. Confusion. Fear. Joy. Vindication. Confusion over why this was happening. Fear of what it meant. Joy that this woman I had genuine fondness for was not actually dead. Vindication? I can't say exactly what had compelled me to sneak back and

---

[5] I have no idea what sort of mushrooms I had set on her, but I guess they must have been edible.

sit vigil on the body, and I wasn't sure what to do now that I had, but all I can say is that sometimes reporting is like jazz: weird hunches and blue notes that sound discordant on their own but help to paint the picture.[6]

Dr. Mag Kenney moved haltingly, like her muscles were stiff and aching. She left the clearing and returned a couple of minutes later with a second backpack, from which she pulled out a mean looking weapon that looked as if it had been created from a bear claw. She used it to slash at the sleeping bag I had laid out for her, shredding it, she then tore up her backpack a little, though not as thoroughly. After that had been done, she stripped to her underwear, before pulling on a set of clothing from the second pack. She then tore up the clothing she had been wearing with the clawed weapon. Finally, she pulled out a mason jar full of what could only be blood, and began applying it liberally to her shredded clothes, in the sleeping bag, and around the spot where I had laid her body. The idea was obviously that by the time the authorities managed to make it out here based on whatever I told them, her body would have already been got at by the various bears, coyotes, and other scavengers that lived in the woods.

When she finished, she took a moment to survey her handiwork, hands on her hips as she looked at the mess that had been made of her corpse. She then surveyed the woods around her, her eyes stopping here and there, and for the life of me I couldn't tell you if we had a flickering moment of eye contact or not. Her survey complete and her death concluded, she

---

[6] What the fuck does that even mean, you hack??? -ed

hitched her second backpack up on her shoulders, and began whistling to herself as she disappeared between the trees.

Why Dr. Kenney felt the need to fake her death, and why she felt the need to include me in her plan were questions I couldn't answer. I had considered saying something, letting her know I was still there, but ultimately I didn't. I let my indecision rule me until it was too late, and she was already gone, vanished back into the forest she loved so much. I guess maybe that wasn't indecision.

I waited another five or ten minutes before sneaking back the way I had come and making the long hike back to my car. The return down the hill and out of the woods was far less pleasant than the walk in had been, as my thoughts piled up like a trainwreck. I found my car unmolested and made my way to the nearest town, where I still couldn't use my cellphone, since it was still cursed, even though I now actually had a signal. There were no payphones, but I found my way to the police station, where I reported that I had found a dead body up on the trail. It took about an hour before an officer would be available, so I went to a diner and had some waffles, which is where I was when the two on-duty police found me. I explained the situation, and showed them the pictures I had taken of the body, then I gave them Dr. Kenney's wallet and phone, and a copy of the map that had got me there. I had to spend far too much time convincing them this wasn't a hoax, and then I had to spend far too much time convincing them that I wasn't the murderer. They literally called up my editor to confirm I was an actual journalist, since the pictures of me by my byline on *The Seattle Picayune* website and even in the physical copy of the paper the diner had a copy of weren't enough evidence without the words of a man to back them up.[7]

By the time they were ready to believe me, it was already far too late in the evening to send out a recovery party, so that would have to wait until the next day, by which time the scavengers would have had a solid chance to get at the dead woman's corpse, just as she had apparently planned. It would actually go on to take a couple of days as the various agencies — local PD, State Police, Forest Service, and for some strange reason the FDA — all argued over who was responsible for recovering the mycologist's body. It was frustrating to observe, but made less frustrating by my knowledge of what they would eventually find, and some part of me felt a warm, mean little glow, knowing that they would blame the missing body on their own stupid squabbles.

I'm not entirely sure why I did it, but I played my part in the charade, alerting the authorities that she had died, then writing and publishing an article about having found Dr. Mag Kenney dead in the woods. I even assisted in writing an obituary, and though I really really wanted to slip in something knowing, I chose not to. *Nobody* fakes their death on a whim, and I didn't want to just wreck whatever plan she was concocting without knowing more about it.

Still, some part of me couldn't help but wonder at myself. After all this strange business with telepathic

[7] Smash the patriarchy.

mushrooms, was it actually me choosing not to say a word of this to anyone, or was it merely what I was being instructed to do. I know that I had been exposed to the cult on at least a couple of occasions. Was it possible that it wasn't me making my decisions? It was an unsettling thought, and I had no real way of answering that question. The same way that an insane person doesn't know that they're insane, right?

I guess at some point this pot will boil over, as they do, and when it comes time for me to tell the whole story, I'll either be able to, or I won't.

And then we'll know.

Kahnaway, thus far:

Jiminy's BigFoot Tours — Jan, 2020

RIP, Granny Snickerdoodle — Feb, 2020

The Kaisershroom — Mar, 2020

Dealer Plates — Apr, 2020

Acornville — May, 2020

The Out Damned Spot Laundromat — Jun, 2020

D.B. Cooper's Underground Opium Emporium — Jul, 2020

Two Cabins — Aug, 2020

Redacted — Sep, 2020

Dick Procyon 4 Mayor —Oct, 2020

The Kahnaway Raccoonteurs —Nov, 2020

Top Ten Murdershrooms — Dec, 2020

A Trip Into Murder — Jan, 2021

Quite A Pickle — Feb, 2021

Li'l Shanky's — Mar, 2021

The America's Celebrities Program — Apr, 2021

How To Kill A Spy — May, 2021

Two Trails — June, 2021

Kahnaway is a serialized novel being published monthly or thereabouts.

Make sure you get every episode by subscribing to Kahnaway at
patreon.com/calavara

Learn more about P. Calavara at Calavara.com and/or NeverKnows.com

Kahnaway — Two Trails: Castor Maléfique Park & Signal Searching
The eighteenth episode of the Kahnaway series

by Polly & Perry Calavara

Kahnaway and Scrivener Jones © 2021
P. Calavara & Never Knows Books

Cover photo by Rick Perry
(the other Rick Perry, not the evil one)

All characters, towns, trails, elves, axes, mushrooms, wounds both physical and emotional, and beavers created by the Calavara Twins™ and they retain all rights, both living and dead, forever and ever, amen.

eighteenth episode, June 2021
First printing, June 2021

ISBN: 978-1-946296-40-5

Never Knows Books is a subsidiary of the Never Knows Heavy Manufacturing Concern

9 781946 296405